IT'S OVER

IT'S OVER

*Nakba-Catastrophe
In Daman*

Byron Daring

iUniverse, Inc.
Bloomington

It's Over
Nakba-Catastrophe
In Daman

iUniverse books may be ordered through booksellers or by contacting:

iUniverse
1663 Liberty Drive
Bloomington, IN 47403
www.iuniverse.com
1-800-Authors (1-800-288-4677)

ISBN: 978-1-4759-5690-0 (sc)
ISBN: 978-1-4759-5691-7 (ebk)

Printed in the United States of America

iUniverse rev. date: 11/07/2012

CONTENTS

SYNOPSIS

The twenty-first century has witnessed protests and revolutions in many countries, most recently in the Arab world (e.g., Tunisia, Egypt, Libya, Syria, Yemen, and several others). This has been popularly dubbed the Arab Spring. Some of the governments running these countries in turmoil have been democratically elected. Others are, and have been, the products of military interventions. "Democratic dictatorships" are the phenomena one sees when leaders, who were initially freely elected, are unwilling to cede power to the changing will of the people.

It is estimated that 10 percent of the Islamic people (over 1.3 billion) are radicals, who would sacrifice their lives to fight for their principles and meet their objectives. Dictators may use these jihadists to further their goals, both internally and internationally. It should be possible to eliminate these dictators and have them replaced with democratic leaders without going to war. The author explains one of many strategies that could successfully depose an unwanted dictator.

CHAPTER 1

ALEX'S MEETING WITH THE ANTI-TERRORIST
INTERNATIONAL ORGANIZATION (ATIO).

A few years ago, Alex Martin, a practicing physician in his midfifties, had developed, directed, and executed a plot that succeeded in eliminating the dictator of Isla Grande (Fito Robles). Ultimately, peace, justice, and democracy were restored as a result of Alex's brilliant plan, which was called the Omega Project. He was the architect of the audacious and unprecedented plot for the removal of the deranged megalomaniac who had presided over the public humiliation and degradation of the very people he professed to protect.

The Anti-terrorist International Organization (ATIO) became aware of the particulars of the Omega Project and had identified Alex and his cohorts as the authors of the well-executed plot. They decided to contact Alex and seek his advice in reference to Anam Hafiz, the ruthless, vicious dictator of Baran, an oil-rich former principality in the Persian

Gulf. Tales emerged of Anam's sanguineous and questionable tastes concerning his nocturnal entertainment. In addition to the brutality with which he treated his numerous concubines, some of whom were little more than girls, he also boasted of his superior pugilistic skills in contests with members of his own sex. Predictably, his opponents, who were selected from members of his own court, would feign stupor upon being hit and fall to the ground senseless. Instead of eliciting suspicions of being mocked, Anam would proudly pound his hairy chest and wax expansive as to his martial prowess. Indeed, he would often tell his retainers in his drunken confidences to direct all political dissenters to his makeshift ring for a proper pummeling. Naturally, this was never followed through. Sometimes he would have his unlucky challengers fight among themselves and would deem the entertainment paltry and insufficient if profuse amounts of blood were not spilled. He seemed to be frustrated that his own contests were so brief. This all explains why so few of his people sought employment in this notable's court, despite the fact that many of them lived in abject poverty.

Covert activities had been carried out by Baranian intelligence, which failed to precipitate the expected internal revolt. Propaganda had been disseminated that Anam had artificially raised the price of basic food staples while secretly disposing of the much-needed food. Small gatherings began to assemble, protesting the outrage, all under the close scrutiny of the ubiquitous surveillance cameras hidden throughout the desert country. When it was discovered that the principal players of this drama would mysteriously "disappear," the resistance lost its vigor, and a concerted opposition became impossible. The occasional perfunctory displays of rebellion were usually expressed through the written word. The authors, once identified, would be brutally tortured and locked up for indefinite periods of time. These exercises were carried out in the spirit of a drill for a possible future crisis, as these writers posed no serious threat to national security, especially given the fact that the majority of the population was functionally illiterate.

When Alex Martin received an unmarked parcel with no return address at his home in Miami Beach, he could well surmise the nature of its contents. The nature of the appeal was lightly skimmed over so that an uninitiated reader could not guess its possible motivation. What was unquestionable was the enclosed first-class round-trip ticket to the Bahamas. These guys must be in a hurry, Alex thought as he noted the postage date.

Alex decided to attend the secret meeting at the Governor's Club, a luxurious resort located on Paradise Island, Bahamas. Three of the top ATIOs, dressed in dark gray suits and tinted sunglasses, met him at a business suite adorned in polished brass and mahogany. Alex was casually dressed in white trousers with a matching guayabera, an embroidered long-sleeved shirt popular among men and women in South Florida, Central America, and the Caribbean.

Alex smiled as he sat in one of the seats arranged around the black lacquered table. Were they trying to intimidate him with their Men in Black personas? If so, they were sorely mistaken. Only one of them, an agent by the name of Ross, thought to identify himself, while the other two remained aloof, showing only an occasional frown. Ross quickly broke the ice.

"Gentlemen, needless to say, this meeting has never officially taken place. Theodore Ross cleared his throat.

"As you say, sir, needless to say. We will dispense with the innumerable minutiae attendant in such meetings and get to the heart of the matter. It need not be pointed out to you, surely, that your work is, shall we say, unconventional. It would not do for word to get out of the myriad breaches of international protocol that your work represents."

Alex chuckled and asked: "Do you gentlemen work for Interpol?"

Ross raised his eyebrows.

"Certainly not, sir. We merely wish to point out the confidential and imperative nature of the matter. You see, the individual we are dealing with is notoriously paranoid. Apart from the usual unsavory chums that such a character collects, delusional power seekers who aspire to world prominence, he has managed to ingratiate himself with some major players."

Alex pondered this as he twirled a silver dollar between the fingers of his right hand.

"Yes, yes. I see your point. This must be handled with great care." As Alex was preparing to elaborate, one of the unidentified agents whispered something into Ross's ear. Ross perked up.

"Perhaps, Mr. Martin, it would be best to discuss this over cocktails on the balcony."

Alex playfully looked under the table's surface, in a furtive search for something suspicious.

"Gentlemen, I'm afraid I mistook you for your superiors."

Ross sharply responded, "As I think I mentioned before, this has all been hastily arranged. You are our contact of last resort."

Alex smiled as he took in a panoramic view of the hotel. "And not a bad resort at that."

After a round of cocktails on the balcony, with the beautiful background of blue calm seas caressing the gorgeous white sandy beach, they described the situation in Baran. The leader of the group, a man easily four inches taller than the rest, finally spoke up.

"Baran is a battered country, located in a critical region of the Middle East. It is sitting on the third-largest reserves of oil in the world. Its government has proven hostile to the West, meaning basically the US and Europe, providing the various indigenous terrorist groups of the region with weapons, soldiers, and intelligence. We want to avoid a war that could well have global ramifications. If you could make arrangements such as you orchestrated in the Omega Project, you will prevent much unneeded bloodshed."

Alex produced a Mont Blanc pen and a small pad. "Are there any international events outside Baran that Anam will be attending?"

Theodore Ross looked at an antique vase as if it contained the answer and responded. "Yes. In the month of July, there will be a meeting of ambassadors and diplomats from around the world hosted by Anam at the Mera Hotel in Daman. Normally, this would be beneath Anam's radar screen, but he's fishing for clients that can provide him with some much needed petrodollars."

Alex tapped his lips with his pen. "Let me think of a plan. I will contact you in the next two weeks."

He rested his head on the back of his chair and gazed at the darkening sky. A balmy breeze was blowing through his thick salt-and-pepper hair. Then he seemed to recall that he had company and sprang to his feet and shook hands with the three agents. He thought it was curious that they all remained anonymous, save for Ross, and that name, in all likelihood, was an alias. Soon, he would think the matter over at his leisure when he returned home.

CHAPTER 2

ALEX'S MEETING WITH SIMON AND HASSAN

Upon his return to South Florida, Alex sketched the strategic plan that would be implemented at the Mera Hotel in Daman during the upcoming international meeting of diplomats. He needed to assemble a crack team of assistants and seek the help of his dear friend and colleague, Dr. Gordon Johnson, chairman of the Department of Anesthesiology at the hospital where he had practiced for many years. He contacted Simon Thomas, who was vacationing in the newly liberated Isla Grande, and Hassan Nader, who had relocated to Nassau, Bahamas. Alex arranged a meeting with both of his associates at the Pearl Cove Resort at West Palm Beach.

The main boulevard leading up to the Mediterranean-style resort was lined with royal palms, with thick groves of native hardwoods at either side. As Alex drove his Mercedes past the gurgling fountain to the valet station and walked into the vestibule, he mentally reviewed all the salient points of his plan. When he crossed the marble-tiled lobby, an attendant quickly escorted him to the conference room. He had always been an esteemed client.

Hassan Nader showed up wearing casual sneakers, white trousers, and a color print shirt. He also sported a deep tan. Simon Thomas wore Levi's and a light short-sleeved shirt. In contrast, Alex was more formally attired in a white shirt and tie. He arrived at the resort after making his rounds at the hospital.

Alex, Simon, and Hassan relived the exhilarating moments of the successfully executed Omega Project. Alex apprised them of his rendezvous with the high-ranking members of the ATIO. He considered various strategies and selected one that was challenging and, if also successfully executed, would eliminate Anam without bloodshed. He explained.

"This project will require the involvement of the three of us. Hassan will provide the initial contact with Anam. He will have to sell the idea of a contest to be held at the Mera Hotel in Daman. He will be our cultural liaison to bait the gullible leader to accept this ploy. Granted, the idea of a physical contest is sophomoric, but given Anam's past history of over-the-top macho displays, this should not be too difficult. I needn't tell you, Hassan, that while you are free to flatter your host in moderation, you must never be fawning. If you make that mistake, you will lose all of his respect and, therefore, his goodwill."

Hassan tugged his curly brown hair in a mock display of frustration.

"Alex, with all due respect, I think I know this neck of the woods better than you."

Alex lifted his open palms.

"Point taken. Simon, you and I will set up the trap, and you must play the part of Anam's instructor. More important than being overly professional, you must not criticize him too much. Whereas he is notoriously gullible, he also has a very fragile ego. We must have appropriate passports and visas that will enable us to participate as delegates to the international meeting. I will expedite the necessary documentation, the equipment that will be utilized, as well as the approval of a budget that will pay our expenses, including compensation for you both. The project will be alternately called It's Over and Nakba, which, as you know, Hassan, means 'catastrophe' in Arabic."

Both Hassan and Simon were intrigued by the project. Hassan was told that he should return to Nassau and wait for ATIO's approval of the completed plan. Simon was asked to be available at any time for a meeting with Alex at the hospital where he worked.

CHAPTER 3

PLANNING PROJECT IT'S OVER (IO)

Alex had spoken to Dr. Gordon Johnson, and a meeting with him and Simon Thomas took place a few days later, on a Saturday morning, in the laboratory at the Department of Anesthesiology.

Alex had requested that Dr. Johnson design a compact air-delivery system that would work underwater. They both had always been ardent scuba divers and practiced their sport on numerous diving expeditions in Florida, the Bahamas, and throughout the Caribbean. After being introduced to Simon, Dr. Johnson produced a mechanism of singular appearance.

"Gentlemen, I wish to direct your attention to the mouthpiece of this contrivance. It is made in such a way as to allow air to be breathed in, with the exhaled air directed via a double-lumen tubing to a container. When exhaling, no air bubbles would surface on the water around the diver. Another important feature is this unique Y connector to the inflow portion of the mouthpiece. At a given time, a one-way valve could be activated, allowing another gas—for instance, helium—to be inhaled by the diver."

Dr. Johnson was not given details of the project when he confessed to a professional curiosity. Alex had told him that he was coordinating underwater experiments that required this special arrangement for air and other gases to be inspired with the exhaled air directed to a container. Bubbles of air would not be visibly exhaled and, therefore, not seen on the water's surface. This was hardly a transparent answer, but the doctor knew better than to press the issue. Alex asked him to have two identical sets made within the next two weeks. He was happy to comply as they had long been colleagues, and he could use the extra money.

"I will call you as soon as they're made."

After leaving Dr. Johnson's laboratory, Simon asked Alex for more details about his plan. Alex smiled at his associate, fraternally. Simon Thomas had begun his service for Dr. Alex Martin as an assistant and medical researcher. He evolved into a sort of man Friday, giving the doctor the benefit of his encyclopedic knowledge, as well as his miscellaneous skills in the applied sciences. Alex had hired him as a young temp and was, frankly, unaware to this day of his educational background.

Alex drove Simon to the marina, where his yacht, already quite familiar to Simon, was moored. They sat comfortably in the teak-lined salon of the boat. The roseate lighting gave the room the cozy feeling of a neighborhood pub. Alex adjusted the air-conditioning and then made them a few rounds of Cuba libres. Alex returned to the plot.

"My plan is to have Hassan convince Anam to participate in a competitive contest that could be held on the roof of the Mera Hotel. Anam was a passionate swimmer as a youth and still fancies himself something of a Poseidon. Naturally, he has become soft around the middle lately, and he no longer swims so gracefully. His lackeys, however, are our best allies, for they dare not tell him so—sort of like the story of the emperor's new suit. Anam could challenge the ambassadors and delegates to a breath-holding contest. I know this sounds insane, but consider the issue of rank. Nobody will think to deny the capricious whims of a powerful head of state. Remember, it behooves these diplomats to humor this volatile madman, as their very careers may suffer if he makes his displeasure known. Of course, he will be shown how to guarantee his victory, so as to save face. We must have a representative of each country jump into the pool and grab a hollow pole in the center of the pool. Fireworks could be launched from this pole as well as the deck. The pole will have handles to allow the diver a firm grasp to remain underwater. We will install a secret port at the base of the pole, through which a mouthpiece will extrude. It will be used by Anam to allow him to breathe undetected and, therefore, assure himself the victory. What nobody will know is that, at a given moment, we will activate a valve that will allow another gas to be inspired by Anam. That gas is cyanide!"

Simon's eyes widened in surprise as he ran his hands through his short blond hair. "What a clever idea. Still, how can you be sure Anam will agree to participate in the event?"

Alex responded, "As I told you, this is where Hassan comes into the picture. He will visit Anam in Baran and explain to him the religious and political impact of this seemingly childish contest. As I have already mentioned, Hassan will know how to masterfully exploit his numerous character defects. Anam fancies himself a cosmopolitan playboy who loves showing off and, therefore, welcomes challenges. In addition to all this, you must remember that his people are frustrated, as they have not seen the fruits of their vast petroleum reserves. He must raise his stature as a cult figure if he is to escape being yet another casualty of the Arab Spring uprisings. When it is explained to him that he will definitely emerge as the winner and thus inspire the admiration of the Arab world as the leader who humiliated representatives of the East and the West, how can he refuse? Besides, you know how convincing Hassan can be. The only thing left is to convince the ATIO of the project's merits. Simon, I want you to give Anam a private demonstration of the device. Later, you and I will arrange for the others to be distracted by a party given in their honor as we secretly set up the equipment. We will go to the floor under the pool to set up the breathing device. You and I will each carry a set of mouthpieces and, if we are questioned, we will explain that we are taking a diving trip to the Red Sea to explore its beautiful coral reefs admired the world over."

Simon requested, "Please tell me about the cyanide."

Alex responded, "Cyanide is a chemical compound that contains what is called the cyano group, which is a carbon atom triple bonded to a nitrogen atom. This chemical arrangement is the lethal weapon which prevents, at the cellular level, the utilization of the oxygen we breathe. Interestingly this compound is produced by certain bacteria, fungi and algae and also found in a number of plants. It is present as well, in small amounts in certain seeds, for example mango, apple, peach and bitter almonds."

Simon interjected, "Cyanide can be detected in the exhaust of internal combustion engines. How is it handled if introduced into a person?"

Alex answered, "It causes what is called histotoxic anoxia. Histo means tissue and anoxia, the lack of oxygen. Therefore oxygen in our tissues cannot be utilized. Our central nervous system and heart are particularly affected.

Oral (by mouth) ingestion of a small quantity, such as 200 ml of cyanide solution and air exposure of 270 ppm (parts per million) may lead to death within minutes.

Hydrogen cyanide released from pellets of Zyklon-B was used extensively in the systematic mass murders of the Holocaust, especially in extermination camps.

Poisoning of hydrogen cyanide gas within a gas chamber (salt of hydrocyanic acid dropped into a strong acid, usually sulfuric acid) is the method of executing a condemned prisoner. The prisoner would breathe the lethal fumes. This is the technique that I will use."

Simon seemed skeptical and said, "How can we bring in the poison?"

Alex replied, "Very simple. A shoemaker, who was my patient a few years ago, has made several shoe molds I use to keep the shape of three pairs which I will be traveling with. One mold has been specially constructed. It is hollow, can be separated in two halves, and the inner lining has a special plastic impermeable to liquids and gases. The contents in a pair of molds are undetectable by any type of screening technique. The mold for my tuxedo pair of shoes will have the salt in one and the acid in the other. To my surprise, my former patient charged me nothing nor asked any questions. He knows I am not a drug dealer. His work was an expression of gratitude because I never charged for my services to him and his wife."

Alex continued, "In the hotel room, I will prepare the cocktail very carefully."

Simon asked, "I understand how you are planning to transport the poison. Assuming we will succeed in introducing it in Daman, how will you prepare the cocktail and administer the gas?"

Alex responded, "I need a large syringe with a Luer-Lok attachment and two 18 gauge needles. I only need one syringe and one needle; the other is a backup. The attachment prevents the escape of the content in the syringe."

Simon wanted more information and asked, "How will you use them?"

Alex responded, "I will prepare the cocktail in the syringe and place it in a long, rectangular case which was used for a necklace. After mixing the two ingredients in the syringe, I will place it and the two 18 gauge needles in the box which I will carry in the pocket of my jacket."

Simon questioned Alex's explanation, "I don't get it. You will introduce the deadly mixture in the breathing system, but how?"

Alex patiently answered, "When Hassan signals through the walkie talkie that Anam has submerged, you will be with me to distract the Arab engineer saying, that they should be ready for the fireworks, which will be released from the central pole. I will connect the loaded syringe to the 18 gauge needle which will puncture the short limb of the Y connector to the pony tank. Anam will be breathing from the large tank. I will disconnect the large tank by closing its valve and opening the valve of the pony tank. The air in this tank will carry the mixture to the mouth piece. After a couple of minutes I will return the original connection to the large tank and get the needle and syringe back into the case and into my pocket.

We will carry the tubing mouthpiece and the pony tank to our room. By this time Anam will be dead."

Again Simon questioned Alex, "How will you bring the large syringe and the 18 gauge needles into the country?"

"We will not carry the syringes and needles," Alex explained, "a member of the US delegation will bring them into the country with several small needles and syringes and insulin. He will indicate that he is diabetic and plans to be in some remote areas after the convention."

Simon then added, "We will have to dispose of the pony tank, tubing, and syringes before we leave the country."

Alex agreed, "We will take care of all of this on our way to the airport."

Simon responded enthusiastically, "Brilliant! What must we do now?"

Alex answered, "We must test the breathing system. I propose we do it at the John Pennycamp Coral Park off Key Largo. We should get together this weekend."

Simon replied, "It's a deal."

On Saturday morning, Alex and Simon sailed toward Key Largo. Around noon they anchored at Carrysfort Reef and put on their wet suits. Alex had two air tanks attached to his vest; one was full with air and the other one empty. The tubing connecting the regulators was specially designed. It had a Y arrangement. The long limb of the tubing had a double lumen and ended at the mouthpiece. Simon jumped into the water to observe Alex in his rehearsal. Alex used the mouthpiece and opened the two regulators' valves; when he inhaled air, it came from the tank filled with air. When he exhaled, the expired air was directed to the empty tank.

The system worked beautifully. Simon watched Alex diving around magnificent corals. No air bubbles came out of the mouthpiece.

Another test was the connection from the pony tank he carried attached to his waist. This tank was connected to the long limb of the tubing. He disconnected the input or air from the large tank and opened the connection to the pony tank. This also was successful.

Alex indicated that the tubing connected to the pony tank could be pierced with an 18 gauge needle.

Close to sunset the testing of the systems was completed.

Simon exclaimed, "Splendid! You obviously have thought of all the details and proven the feasibility of all the steps. Are we carrying tanks with us?"

Alex replied, "No, I will buy two tanks from a dive shop in Danam: One large tank will be filled with air, and the other tank empty. I will also buy a pony tank which will also be filled with air. You and I will carry two mouthpieces, regulators, tubing with valves, and the usual diving gear (wetsuits, masks, snorkels, vests and fins). In Daman we will rehearse. We also have plenty of time to talk during our long trip to Daman."

Simon asked, "How can we attend this meeting? It is exclusively for the diplomats and their staff."

Alex answered Simon's question clearly: "We will travel as members of the U.S. delegation. ATIO will provide us with the necessary documentation. You and I will meet with Hassan again after I get the go-ahead." They docked around 7:00 p.m. and went home.

On Monday, Alex called his contacts at the ATIO. He was told to return to the Bahamas. This time they met at a more prosaic resort. Alex knew that counter-intuitively, this was actually a good sign. He had a sample of the diving mouthpiece. His meeting was with the tall imposing figure who had held back in their initial meeting. He identified himself as Frank Schmidt and he was obviously in charge. This time, the other two held back. After explaining his plan in detail, Alex requested the proper documentation for himself, Simon, and Hassan. It seems the agents of the ATIO had already run character and personal reference checks on Alex and Simon. Hassan Nader, however, was under their radar screen. Alex indicated that without Hassan, the success of the mission could not be assured. He elaborated further that both Hassan and Simon should be paid $500,000 each for their service upon the completion of the project. Agent Frank

Schmidt placed a call from a room adjacent to the living room of the suite. He emerged 15 minutes later and said, "Alex, you have an incredibly good reputation. All your requests have been approved. You and Simon Thomas will travel as members of the U.S. delegation. You will share a suite at the Mera Hotel in Daman. I'm afraid Mr. Nader must make his own arrangements. It is our understanding that he will travel first to Baran to arrange a meeting with Anam. If he is successful, he will then notify you and rendezvous with you and Simon in Daman. We will honor your request for the compensation of your partners. Naturally, you cannot carry any documents related to the project."

After a pause, he resumed, "Alex, is there anything you need?"

Alex responded, "Yes, the head of the US delegation, Mr. Matthew Reed, must bring to Daman several vials of insulin, small syringes, and two large syringes, plus a couple of 18 gauge needles. He will justify these by indicating that he is a diabetic and may take side tours to some remote locations."

"Alex, what will you get out of this? As far as I can tell, you are not seeking any remuneration."

Alex bit his lip. "Since the assassination of my wife by a cruel dictator, who is no longer alive, I promised myself I would be instrumental in the elimination of similar dictators. This is akin to a religious vow. I, therefore, will accept no monetary compensation."

The three agents looked at each other in perplexity. Alex furrowed his brow, rose, shook hands with them, and left the room.

As soon as he returned to his hotel room, he called Hassan. Alex cupped his hands to the receiver.

"Hassan, I've received the green light to proceed. I'll be right over; don't go anywhere."

Alex took a taxi to Hassan's condo, a two-story structure surrounded by lush tropical foliage, conveniently situated in a quiet cul-de-sac. He found Hassan lounging comfortably in the living room. He had made a pot of coffee in preparation for their brainstorming session. Alex took the lead.

"As I told you before, you will receive $500,000 after the successful completion of the project. You must travel to Baran and ingratiate yourself with Anam through your powerful connections in the region. If you are able to achieve a rapport with Anam, something I know you can do with great facility, you must next convince him of the viability of the poolside contest. Ask him for a reasonable fee in exchange for your work in organizing the event. This will make the whole charade seem legitimate in his eyes, as he attaches great symbolic significance to money. Ask for his assistance, and request the additional support of two experts you trust, namely Simon and myself. We will get together in Daman, if you are instructed to proceed."

Hassan put down his coffee cup and smiled. "Alex, it all seems so easy for you. Frankly, I still don't understand all the details. Can you please go over with me, point by point, all the steps of the IO project?"

Alex held up his hands. "That can wait. I just want to make sure we are not sending you on a wild-goose chase."

"Don't worry about that. I still have a diplomatic passport from Alcania and have a good reputation as an entrepreneur and power broker in the region. Watch me get an additional $500,000 from Anam himself in the process. You know I can do it, just like I did with the Omega Project."

Alex could not help but laugh. "You are so shrewd and clever. I know how convincing you can be. Incidentally, whatever happened to your fiancée, Eva?"

"She is doing fine and is as beautiful as ever. I will ask her to join me on this pleasure trip. She has just returned from visiting her family and is resting by the pool. Let's ask her to join us."

Alex demurred. "No, no, please don't bother. I must be going anyway. Hasta luego."

Hassan Nader joined his young, nubile fiancée by the pool.

"My dear, we have been together now for several years. What don't we know about each other as well as the world? We have traveled all over Europe, Asia, the Americas, and even the Bahamas. I know you must be tired from all this globe-trotting, but I have business to tend to in Baran, and later in Daman, and I cannot bear to be without you. You will have the opportunity to see two different and exciting countries. I promise you will enjoy them both."

Eva winked as she set her margarita down. "You have always filled my life with pleasant surprises. I feel this will be another. Certainly, I'll join you."

Hassan sent an e-mail the following day to the ambassador of Alcania in Baran, requesting an hour-long meeting alone with Anam. The subject of the e-mail was "An Offer You Can't Refuse." Three days later, Hassan was notified that a meeting could take place in three weeks at the Royal Palace in Baran. Hassan rushed to the bedroom, kissed Eva ardently, and said, "Start planning your schedule. In three weeks you must have your things packed and ready because we will be flying to Baran—oh, and don't forget your thongs."

CHAPTER 4

HASSAN'S VISIT WITH ANAM IN BARAN

Baran is a very rich country that supplies oil to many countries around the world. Most of these countries are in the Pacific Rim. However, due to recent geopolitical trends, more and more Western nations have expressed an interest in becoming its client. There is a marked contrast between the crumbling old buildings, some little more than mud brick structures, and the modern shiny skyscrapers of glass and steel. The downtown district is the scene of a perpetual traffic jam of cars, buses, and trucks. Most of the few tourists that venture here hail from other Arab countries.

Politically, the country has been ruled by Shiite leaders who have appointed nonmiltary Baranians to key posts in the government. The affairs of state are conducted by secular ministers in contrast to other countries in the region. Though a former principality, the hereditary succession has long been allowed to lapse, and a series of strongmen have taken their place. Though ostensibly Islamic, these leaders have not displayed remarkable piety. On the contrary, their ostentatious lifestyle has kept the populace in a destitute condition in a country of immense natural wealth. Anam Hafiz has dutifully maintained this tradition.

The bazaars and street markets display antique rugs as well as their modern mass-produced cousins. Jewelry, handicrafts, and numerous stalls offering a sampling of the local fare provide a potpourri for the senses. Eva Velez enjoyed herself shopping, as the restrictions placed on women throughout the Gulf were nonexistent in Baran, and what few restrictions might exist in forgotten statutes were never enforced.

When Hassan arrived with Eva to greet the ambassador of Alcania, a tall bald man with a Roman nose, they were conveyed to the luxurious Emerald Sea Hotel. The following morning, Hassan was driven by a court chauffeur to the Royal Palace, where he was greeted by Anam himself. The Gulf leader was dressed in a white linen suit and had his two bejeweled hands resting contentedly on his huge barrel-shaped torso. Apparently, he had just finished an enjoyable and satisfying repast. He surveyed his guest with a somnolent but inquisitive gaze. Scarlet-uniformed guards were posted at the main entrance, foyer, and in front of every door. The marble façade matched the floor and made Hassan think of the Taj Mahal.

Hassan was thoroughly checked for weapons and other metal objects. He was then escorted to the Blue Room, featuring ornamental tiles and filigree of masterful excellence. This is where Anam conducted all his official government affairs. After exchanging trivial anecdotes, Hassan explained the purpose of his visit.

"Your Highness, you will be hosting the first multiethnic international meeting at the Mera Hotel in Daman. I would like to propose an original contest that you will inevitably win.

Your triumph will show once more how powerful you are and indirectly highlight the leadership of Arabs in the world. I want you to contract me to organize this event."

Anam replied, "I am very intrigued by your remarks and most anxious to learn the features of this contest."

Hassan spread his hands before him as if to pan the room.

"A cocktail party to entertain all the ambassadors and delegates attending the meeting will take place on the roof of the hotel, around a centrally located pool. I suggest you provide the attendants with music, beautiful dancers, and fireworks. It would be helpful if the entertainment was of a typical Baranian nature, as this would serve to brand your prestige on the occasion. A central fountain in the pool will serve a dual purpose. In addition to a water fountain, its hollow center will release fireworks at the appropriate moment."

Anam raised his eyebrows. "Why are you stressing so many details about the pool area?"

Hassan explained, "Without the central column in the pool, you cannot win the contest."

Anam motioned him with his right hand. "Please continue."

"When the party begins, you will announce that there will be a contest. Every delegation will assign a representative to jump into the pool, swim toward the central pole, and, when instructed, take a deep breath and dive. There will be handles on the surface of the pole that the diver can grab. A large clock with a chronometer will mark how long the diver was able to hold his breath. A billboard will display the name of the country represented by the diver, his name, and the time of his dive. Upon the completion of each diver's dive, fireworks will explode to great fanfare."

Anam shrugged his shoulders. "Where does that leave me?"

"You will be the master of ceremony and therefore the last to dive."

Anam frowned. "Whereas I am fond of water sports and am physically able to perform deeds of a man half my age, I do not enjoy disrobing in public. Perhaps some people will imagine I am out of shape."

Hassan smiled solicitously. "Nonsense, you are as fit as a bull. But let me finish describing the event. You will surprise the crowd by challenging all comers and offering valuable prizes to the winner: a Rolls-Royce and a week at the Jumeirah Hotel in Dubai, with chauffeur, servants, and beautiful women to serve all the needs of the champion. However, I haven't told you everything about the central pole in the swimming pool. At the base of the pole there will be a small hidden hatch from which a tube with a special mouthpiece will protrude. Here it is." He showed Anam the small mouthpiece. "The arrangement will only be used by you. When you dive, you will hold on to a handle of the pole, activate the release of the mouthpiece, and discreetly place it in your mouth. You will gently breathe in and out. You can remain underwater for hours."

Anam waved his bejeweled right hand in a show of dismissal. "The viewers will discover the trick because bubbles of exhaled air will surface."

Hassan protested. "Not true. I have prepared this mouthpiece and breathing system just for you. As you exhale the air, a conduit in the double-lumen tube will transport the exhaled air to a container under the floor of the pool, at the base of the pole. I will contract a highly responsible team for the installation. We will show you how the system works and familiarize you with the use of the breathing system. Naturally, this will all be kept secret. Can you imagine what this means, to beat all the participants? You may even break the Guinness record for holding one's breath, if such a thing exists. We would encourage you to call the people at Guinness to make it official. You would then pooh-pooh such publicity and thereby establish your modesty and magnanimity."

Anam beamed. "All you have said sounds interesting. You are a very astute businessman. I have checked your credentials and know that you are very competent. How much do you want to organize and execute this project?"

Hassan joined the fingers of both of his hands.

"I leave my compensation up to your generosity. I would suggest that you provide me with $500,000 before the event and, upon successfully winning the contest, another $500,000. I will take care of the expenses of my team. You must instruct your personnel to trust me, telling them I am a very important person and one of your close allies. I need a couple of weeks before the meeting to prepare the scenario. Two days before the party, you will be trained in the use of the breathing system. No one can know about this plan. My fiancée and I will be visiting Baran for a week. Let me know about your decision. This is a win-win situation for you, Your Highness, as well as the Arab world. Imagine the publicity you will get in every friendly, and even unfriendly, nation! Whether official or not, the thought of you breaking the Guinness World Record will be like winning the Nobel Prize!"

Hassan shook hands with Anam and was taken aback when the big man embraced him and kissed him on both cheeks in a warm display of affection. He tried not to smile as he left the palace. Three days later, he received a sealed envelope. It had $300,000 and a note that read, "Proceed as planned. You will get the second installment after the rehearsal."

Hassan jumped up and down like a child as Eva watched him, bemused. When he told her the news, she congratulated him, and later that evening they celebrated at a luxurious restaurant. The following afternoon (it was morning in the eastern US), Alex received a call from Hassan. He said, "I'll meet you in Daman two weeks before the meeting. We have received the okay."

CHAPTER 5

ORGANIZATION OF THE PLAN AT THE
MERA HOTEL IN DAMAN

In Washington, Alex met the chairman of the American delegation, the Honorable Douglas Edwards, a bespectacled older gentleman with sharp blue eyes and a patrician demeanor. After introducing Alex, he explained that they had been contracted for a mission and Alex and Simon would be traveling as members of the security force of the American delegation. No details were offered about the mission. It could be assumed that someone high up was calling in a favor to allow these intelligent but innocuous agents to attend the international meeting. They were not subjected to the third-degree questioning that was considered de rigueur on such occasions and were viewed by the delegation with an almost condescending benevolence. This is precisely what Alex wanted, as he was not interested in the tedious minutiae of diplomatic protocol.

A week before the International Affairs Congress was to begin, Alex and Simon flew from New York to Daman and checked into the five-star Mera Hotel. The delegates and ambassadors had not yet arrived. Hassan and Eva checked in the same afternoon.

Daman is one of the wealthiest Arab countries in the world. There are several magnificent hotels and imposing skyscrapers of avant-garde architectural designs. Many shopping malls with big-name stores exhibit their latest merchandise. In addition, there are many upscale boutiques that would be more familiar to their well-heeled Asian clients. Artificial islands have been designed by foreign personnel that represent cheap labor, in comparison with Damanian standards. Lessons have been learned from the Israeli experience of reclamation of desert lands. Farms and golf courses, as well as plush manicured gardens, are commonplace in this opulent land. Stately mansions are safely ensconced in well-guarded walled communities. One sees Rolls-Royces, Mercedes-Benzes, Lamborghinis, Ferraris, and every other luxury car imaginable featuring not only sublime aesthetics but superior engineering. All manner of beautiful yachts are docked at the packed marinas lining the harbor. Most are owned by very wealthy Arabs.

Hassan contacted Alex, and a meeting was set for the same evening. Hassan, Alex, and Simon ordered their dinner from room service. When the waiter had served the assembled guests and left, Hassan began.

"Our friend has agreed to all aspects of the project. You both have to get busy first thing tomorrow with the Department of Engineering, which is in charge of all the mechanical and electrical arrangements."

Alex elaborated. "Yes, I know. They must install the special central pole. Luckily, we already provided them with the engineering blueprints, as you instructed us to do, using your name, obviously. Simon and I must check the pole and install the breathing system. We will say that it may be necessary to use it, in the event the diver is in need of air. We will stress that it is only an emergency precaution. We will keep the mouthpiece and the double-lumen tube in our room till the last moment, as well as the 'special herbs.' Hassan, you must introduce us as your hired staff to assist in the contest. I am sure you will say we are mercenaries with special 'plumbing' skills. We will place a hole at the base of the pole, through which the mouthpiece will be deployed. The Arab workers will not be told of this and, naturally, will not witness the maneuver. Fortunately, both devices are small enough to fit in our pockets. There will be two tanks, one filled with air and the other one empty. The latter will collect the exhaled air of our diver."

The following morning, Hassan, Alex, and Simon met the chief engineer, who escorted them to the floor below the swimming pool. A hole had been drilled to accommodate the large hollow pole. Fireworks and water could traverse the pole through its double tubing. Handles were installed on the sides of the pole to facilitate the stabilization of the divers as they hold their breaths. After a full day's work and testing of the equipment, they called it a day. The following morning, Alex would test the system.

The morning after their arrival, Alex visited a sports store that sold diving equipment. He bought two large-capacity diving tanks and a small pony tank, which is usually attached to a belt and has enough air for about fifteen minutes. All were filled with air except one of the large tanks.

That evening, Alex visited Lieutenant Reed of the U.S. Delegation in his room at the hotel. He gave Alex two large syringes and two 18 gauge needles. In his room at the hotel

Alex carefully disassembled the hollow mold inside his tuxedo shoes and removed the bags containing the poison. The pellets were placed first in the barrel of one of the syringes which had a stop valve to prevent any leak. Alex covered his nose with a wet towel and proceeded to introduce the acid. He quickly inserted the plunger of the syringe and allowed for space for the expanding gas. The loaded syringe was placed in the long, rectangular box which also contained two 18 gauge needles. One was a backup. The case was carried in one of the pockets in his jacket.

Alex explained, "I will have the pony tank connected to the air-containing large tank. Hassan, when Anam jumps in the water, Simon should come down and join me. He will distract the Arab engineers, saying to them that they must be prepared for the fireworks. This will give me the time to connect the pony tank to the tubing that leads to the tank supplying the air. When Hassan signals again this will indicate that Anam is by the pole breathing under water. I will be able to confirm this by observing the flow of exhaled air into the empty tank.

I will open the box I will be carrying in my pocket, attach the needle to the Luer-Lok valve in the syringe, pierce the tubing connecting the pony tank (the short limb of the Y connection), empty the syringe, close the valve of the large tank, and simultaneously open the valve of the pony tank. Anam will inhale the "cocktail" which will be advanced towards the mouthpiece by the pressurized air of the pony tank. After three minutes I will disconnect the system, close all the valves, retrieve the tubing attached to the mouthpiece, put back the syringe in my pocket, and ask the engineer to start the fireworks. Simon, you and I will leave the scene carrying all the equipment including the tubing, the regulators, and the pony tank. The only things we will leave behind are the two large tanks."

Hassan asked, "We can understand all the steps but what will you do with all the equipment?"

Alex replied, "We will put everything in our luggage as we brought them to Danam. Remember we planned for a diving trip in the Red Sea. I will dispose of the large syringes and needles on our way to the airport."

The next day before dawn, Simon showed up on the pool deck. Alex went to the floor under the pool. Only one Arab employee was with him. He spoke very little English and knew nothing of what was going on. Hassan showed up on the pool deck a while later with a walkie-talkie. Alex had another and the reception was clear. Hassan greeted Simon and asked him if he was ready.

Simon replied, "Ready to go." He jumped into the climatized, impeccably clean swimming pool. He swam towards the central pole, took a dive, and surfaced a few seconds later.

Hassan smiled: "Ready for the real dive?"

Simon answered, "Here I go." He took a deep breath and dove to the bottom of the pole. He pushed a button, which opened a small hole. The mouthpiece and tube appeared. Simon fitted the mouthpiece to his mouth and started breathing slowly. As he exhaled, the air went was collected in the empty air tank. Everything worked perfectly.

After four minutes under the water, Simon tapped the pole. This was the cue for Alex to disconnect the mouthpiece and retract the system. Simon surfaced and the workers, not knowing of the underwater ventilation apparatus, applauded. Hassan discreetly left the pool deck and returned to his suite. That evening, Hassan and Eva celebrated with Alex and Simon. They had begun to really appreciate each other's company.

Everything worked as expected. They reviewed the checklist. The pole was in place. It allowed the fountain to function properly, as well as permitting the release of the fireworks. The handles were in place. The secret hatch for the release system for the mouthpiece and double-lumen tube was operational. The recirculating air-exchange system functioned properly. Now they were ready for the pool trial with Anam.

CHAPTER 6

REHEARSAL AT THE SWIMMING POOL

Anam was contacted by Hassan. They agreed to meet at the pool deck the following morning at sunrise. Only Anam's personal guards, Hassan, and Simon were allowed on the pool deck. Alex and an Arab engineer were active on the floor below the pool, where the pole had been installed. The principal role of the engineer was to operate the fountain. He and a technician would also manage the system of fireworks the next morning. Alex was in charge of the two air tanks and the breath-support device.

Anam showed up on time. Hassan smiled as he considered this seemingly insignificant detail.

"Good morning, Your Highness. I hope you are feeling well today."

"Is this a friend of yours?"

Hassan introduced Simon as an expert diver hired by him as a personal instructor to accompany Anam in the pool.

Anam was impressed by Simon's athletic features. His tanned physique betrayed his fondness for outdoor sports.

"Your Highness, everything will work out fine. I have been doing this for years, and I will walk you through the process so that it becomes second nature."

Simon jumped into the pool and asked Anam to follow him to the pole. He gave Anam a swim mask so that he could familiarize himself with the location of the handles and, more importantly, the button at the base of the pole that released the mouthpiece and the double-lumen tube. Simon dove first and asked Anam to watch him closely. He carefully illustrated where the handles and the secret button were located. He asked his host to dive several times without activating the air-support mechanism. Afterward, he showed Anam what happened when the secret button was pressed. He was surprised to see the mouthpiece and tube appear. He could not see Simon putting the mouthpiece on, and his face covered the breathing apparatus completely. He remained motionless. Obviously, Simon was breathing slowly, and yet no bubbles of air appeared. After four to five minutes, Simon pulled the tube gently out of his mouth. This was the prearranged signal for Alex to turn the breathing mechanism off and retract the mouthpiece and tube.

It was Anam's turn to practice with the simulated breath-holding device. He seemed somewhat clumsy in his initial attempts at identifying the secret button and retrieving the mouthpiece. He refused to use the mask. After numerous trials, he was finally able to accomplish the exercise and was slowly breathing in and out. He surfaced after about five minutes and looked happily at his watch. It was clear to him that he could easily beat the diver with the best recorded time under the water. He, of course, had the advantage of being the last to dive.

Anam jumped out of the water and embraced and kissed Hassan on both cheeks again.

"Tonight, you will receive the second payment of our deal. I am very happy."

That evening, Hassan received an envelope containing $200,000. He celebrated that night with Eva.

CHAPTER 7

INSTALLATION OF THE DELIVERY SYSTEM

Hassan, Alex, and Simon met at Alex's suite and went over the plan in great detail. Alex explained everything. He was repetitious, but it was necessary.

"At 1700 hours, I will go with Simon to our station under the swimming pool. We will be carrying the two breathing sets, including the pony tank. We must make sure that the gas can be infused without any leaks. I will carry the syringe with the cocktail in my pocket. Simon and I will make sure that all the connections function properly. There is a Y connection between the tube with the mouthpiece and each of the two tanks. As you know, the one-way valves must function properly so that the air from the air tank goes to the mouthpiece, and the exhaled air goes to the empty tank.

"Hassan, when you say 'now' into your walkie-talkie, I will connect the syringe in my jacket to the tube responsible for the intake of air. As the gas is concentrated, it will require less than a minute to exert its effects. When I say 'two,' you must return with Eva to your suite. You should have your luggage packed beforehand so as to be able to leave the hotel and go to the airport right away.

"As soon as Simon and I complete the inspection of all the connections, he will change and go to the pool deck. There, he will reassure Anam that nothing will go wrong, and he will be there to assist him if necessary. Simon will join me as soon as Hassan jumps into the pool.

"Hassan, you and Eva will attend the party. Make sure you have your walkie-talkie charged. We should test our communication system. Remember, I will not be aware of what is going on in the swimming pool area. I totally depend on the audio link between us. You will say 'now,' instructing me to connect the syringe to the breathing system. Upon completion of the operation, I will say 'two.' You and Eva must immediately leave the deck area and return to your respective rooms. Simon and I will have prepacked our belongings and checked out of the hotel. You must also be ready to leave the hotel promptly. As you know, we have already contracted for transportation to the airport, where we will see each other again. Any questions?"

Hassan looked to Alex's feet. "Have you retrieved the containers from your shoes?"

Alex nodded. "Yes, they arrived safely from America."

Simon seemed nervous. "How will we dispose of the mouthpieces, tubing, regulators, and syringes?"

Alex reassured him. "I will carry the two sets of mouthpieces with their connecting tubing with me, also the pony tank. Remember our cover story. We are divers, and we brought this gear with us, as well as our wet suits and masks, to dive in the coral reefs of the Red Sea. The two boxes will be quickly returned and secured to the two molds of my shoes. It seems we will not be subjected to any aggressive screening at the airport due to our special status as guests."

They exchanged trivial remarks uneasily, as they seemed tense and edgy. They were about to execute a dangerous task. They were not only concerned with their own personal safety but with the possibility of a smooth transition from a brutal regime for Baran and its people. If successful, important changes would occur for this beleaguered population. Already, progressive forces were poised to assume the reins. The world would be a better place without Anam.

Simon tried to cheer up Alex and Hassan.

"Compared to the Omega Project, this is a piece of cake. I hope our next job will be more challenging. As with some Olympic events, we will be judged and rewarded by the difficulty, artistry, and execution."

Though this seemed like whistling in the dark, they all laughed, and Alex and Simon bade Hassan good-bye.

CHAPTER 8

PARTY AT THE SWIMMING POOL

Thursday was the last day of the congress. In the social program, a farewell party with exciting surprises had been announced. All the ambassadors and delegates were requested to attend. In reality, this was only a formality, as most of the guests attending the summit could talk of little else. There was the general expectation that something novel would take place that night.

At sunset, the ambassadors and delegates, in formal dress, walked on the deck of the centrally located swimming pool. A large diving board had been installed at the south end of the deck, under a large clock. Most of the guests felt that these sporting ornaments were out of place. Some even inquired if an internationally sanctioned competition had just taken place and the hotel staff had not been able to remove the equipment on time. To this, the servers smiled good-naturedly and explained that the hotel was accustomed to all manner of extemporaneous contingencies, and the guests were assured that the significance of these objects would soon become apparent.

Torches were lit on the four ends of the deck, and a band played international music. That is to say, music that was popular in different parts of the world. No bias was shown for any particular region. Belly dancers charmed the audience. They invited the men and women present to learn belly dancing, with often clumsy but lighthearted attempts as a result. A podium had been installed next to the billboard. From its height, there was a magnificent view of the spectacularly lighted city. The sunset was a glorious vision of the golden sun gently descending to a pool of red, ochre, and magenta light. Some of those present let out a collective gasp. A coolness that was not uncomfortable pervaded the night.

Arab waitresses carried trays with tasty hors d'oeuvres to refresh the guests. At sunset, the first set of fireworks was launched from the edge of the deck and from the central pole in the pool, where a fountain displayed water arches of varying heights.

Occidental visitors came in their customary tuxedos. Their wives and companions, however, wore long stylish gowns designed by some of the world's top ateliers. The Oriental dignitaries exhibited a variety of silk shirts, capes, and turbans. Their spouses covered their faces with silk masks. Their beautiful black eyes and smooth hands were the only visible parts of their bodies. Others, of a more secular bent, were dressed very much as the Western women were.

Hassan and Eva appeared in their usual remarkable attire. Eva wore a tastefully cut black silk dress, with a contrasting pearl necklace, sapphire earrings, and a diamond bracelet. Anam greeted them as well as his instructor, Simon, who was handsomely dressed in a white suit with matching shoes. With his deep tan, he exuded an air of confidence and health. They smiled, and Simon bowed as a sign of respect.

Several buffet tables redolent with delicacies were set around the pool. White-clothed tables, with a seating capacity of ten each, also surrounded the swimming pool. At the center of each table, the flag and name of each delegation appeared. The plates and silverware displayed Arabian icons.

The celebration had an ambience of luxury, abundance, exquisite good taste, and judicious aesthetics. It was a feast for the eyes, as well as the other senses. Fireworks were launched intermittently after sunset. On the top of each hour, large umbrellas of fireworks were launched from the center of the pool.

CHAPTER 9

THE CONTEST BEGINS

A little after midnight, Anam approached the podium and addressed the group. His fleshy face was flush with the excitement of hosting the summit's festivities, as well as partaking of its refreshments. He raised his outstretched hands with a benevolent smile. The music, the fireworks, and the serving of food abruptly stopped. He had a spotlight directed on him. The only other sources of light were the exit signs and the starry, moonlit night. He spoke with a stentorian voice.

"Welcome to this small paradise on earth. We hope you all enjoy the Arab hospitality customary in this part of the world. We have succeeded at our meeting on airing our differences respectfully and coming to the conclusion that only through peace, tolerance, and understanding can we properly address our disagreements and achieve mutual cooperation. Now I would like to announce a big surprise that will have you remember this night for the rest of your lives. We want you to open your minds to an unconventional form of entertainment. We must all remember not to take ourselves too seriously and always remain young at heart. We want to propose a contest, and we hope that each delegation will select a representative with 'good lungs.' This will be an endurance contest, and we want to give a special prize to the person with the greatest breath-holding capacity. Each competitor will swim toward the center of the pool and, when a signal is given, submerge and hold their breath for as long as they can. I will now display a board with the name of each delegation in alphabetical order. We only need the name of each representative. Note the clock above the board. The chronometer will start at the beginning of the dive and will stop when the diver surfaces. The number of minutes and seconds will appear after the name of each diver. When the contest finishes, we will announce the winner. He will receive several awards: a Rolls-Royce, a weeklong stay at the executive suite of the Jumeirah Hotel in Dubai with a group of attendants, including quite charming ones, and many other things. These unforgettable gifts are given to properly recognize the champion. You have fifteen minutes to select your representative. We have a collection of new swimsuits in the gymnasium adjacent to the swimming pool. I realize that each of you is likely to select the most youthful and most athletic among your staff. Whereas my men, who, after all, are the lions of the Persian Gulf, have no trouble in answering the call to national duty, I have decided to represent the sovereign nation of Baran myself. The show will start in forty-five minutes." With that, he raised his bejeweled hands as if to administer a benediction.

There was a huge silence at first, as the assembled guests looked to one another for help. This was followed by a steady applause, and, finally, a standing ovation. All appeared enthusiastic, particularly the Arab delegations. The music, fireworks, and food service resumed. An Arab attendant approached each table and wrote the name of the selected representative. All the delegations participated. A "judge" collected the names, which were promptly displayed on the board. All the representatives, including Anam, moved to the gymnasium and reappeared in swimsuits. Clearly there were freshman participants who suppressed their smiles only after the most concerted efforts. Clearly, Anam was the least agile among them, though his torso displayed a vaguely bearlike brawn.

The ambassador from the United States, Douglas Edwards, however, approached Anam with no appearance of mirth. "Would you have any objections if my wife represents the American contingent?"

Anam, though surprised, reacted quickly. "Most certainly not. This will prove that Baran is very democratic and, as such, does not tolerate discrimination."

Jane Edwards, the ambassador's wife, was a former Olympic gold medalist in three swimming events. She went to her room and returned in a white Olympic swim outfit. Several Arab leaders exchanged quizzical looks and protested to Anam. "Women cannot participate in a men's event."

Anam replied, "This is a meeting of the International Affairs Organization. We owe our respect to all who are here. This pool is symbolically international territory and, as such, enjoys the rights and privileges of a foreign embassy. Let us be courteous and reasonable. I have decided to represent Baran. I will be just another competitor of the many here. Only because I am the host will I be the last to dive."

Anam went to the microphone and addressed the general assembly. "Let's have a dry run. I will ask one of my assistants to give you a demonstration."

He turned to Simon, who was already dressed in swimming trunks, and motioned for him to give the crowd a demonstration. Simon jumped into the pool and swam toward the pole. He waved his hands to the audience. Hassan gave the signal to start, and a gong was heard. Simon took a deep breath and went under the water. The chronometer began to display the seconds in LEDs. After two and a half minutes, he surfaced and the clock stopped. As soon as the chronometer posted the results, everyone applauded.

Anam explained, "The reason we submerge by the pole is because it has handles that can be grabbed to facilitate our dive. The diver will be in full view of everyone. If anyone present has any questions, I will do my best to elucidate further." The only sound was a general murmur. Anam nodded. "Very well, then. Let the contest begin."

One by one, each diver went underwater and surfaced. The delegate from Switzerland, a tall Nordic type with a barrel-chested body like that of Johnny Weissmuller, had the record time of four minutes and twenty seconds. Next came the delegate from the United States. Everyone admired her beautiful body. She was tall and blonde and also lithe and limber in her movements. Her physique combined the characteristics of a world-class competitive athlete with the graceful lines of a ballerina.

There was absolute silence. Jane jumped into the pool without making a splash. Her swimming was both stylish and efficient. She approached the pole, greeted the audience, and submerged after the sound of the gong. One, two, three, four minutes elapsed. The audience was in suspense. After an additional forty-five seconds, she surfaced. Four minutes, forty-five seconds! She now held the record. Spontaneous applause and ovations greeted her. Regardless of whatever scruples some of the delegates may have had about allowing a female participant, they begrudgingly admired this woman. It was uncontestable. She had bested all the men who had competed before her. She stepped out of the pool and rushed to her husband. The ambassador hugged her and covered her body with a large white towel. He waved to the crowd. Anam approached the microphone with an enigmatic smile.

"We apparently have a winner, who will be very difficult to defeat. Nevertheless, I must not be discouraged. I must, as the Americans say, be a good sport. Therefore, without further ado, I will take my turn, come what may."

CHAPTER 10

ANAM'S DIVE

Simon slowly approached the door to the exit stairwell. His heart was beating so fast that he wondered if the gathered dignitaries could see it pumping through his skin. Hassan and Eva moved close to the main entrance.

After a dramatic flourish of his hands, Anam jumped into the pool and swam slowly toward the central pole, where he stopped and waved to the audience. There were robust cheers, and some delegations even gave him standing ovations. He heard some Arabs shout, "Anam, you can win! Go for it!" Anam waved his hands for several more seconds and then took his dive. The sound of people talking slowly dissipated.

On the pool deck, Hassan surreptitiously said, "Now," into his walkie-talkie. He kept his eye on his fiancée and was encouraged by her cool demeanor. Alex made sure he could see the release of the mouthpiece and tubing thirty seconds from the time of Anam's dive. He knew that Anam was comfortably breathing, unnoticed by the audience. The ruthless dictator must have been thinking of his assured, vain, glorious conquest of all the international competitors, particularly the attractive American. After a minute, Alex connected the syringe to the inlet of the air access tube and temporarily stopped the flow of air from the large tank. He had instructed the Arab personnel to prepare the last group of fireworks. These pyrotechnics would rise in mushroom-cloud formations, with some screeching streakers that would burn out harmlessly but disorient the guests. This allowed Alex to proceed unnoticed with the release of the cyanide.

Simon walked down the exit stairs to the floor below. He was calmer now that he was alone. As he got into an elevator, some tourists saw him dressed in a bathing suit, holding his drink, and waved at him. They must have thought he was drunk, surely some German or American neophyte delegate still not versed in diplomatic etiquette. He joined Alex and followed his instructions.

Hassan slipped into an elevator with Eva. She simulated that she was suffering the effects of rich food and alcohol. Anam's security staff smiled. "What can one expect from a vixen so provocatively dressed?" The couple arrived at their suite, quickly packed their formal wear, and emerged in their street clothes. They got back into the elevator, crossed the lobby, and entered a chauffeured limousine that would drive them to the airport.

Alex put the syringe back in his pocket and disconnected the tubing. He packed the mouthpieces and then spoke to the engineering assistants. He told them to prepare the fireworks and grand finale. They had no knowledge of what had happened in the pool. Naturally, these workers were little noticed as they played a purely ancillary role in the night's entertainment and were, therefore, kept uninformed of vital matters.

Alex and Simon walked out and rode an elevator to their suite.

Both changed clothes and finished packing their luggage.

As the luggage was already almost completely packed, Alex just had to change his clothes and insert the boxes in the supports of his shoes. They did not talk any further. Their TV set showed the deck of the pool and people frantically running around. Alex motioned to Simon, and they slipped out of the room like cat burglars.

CHAPTER 11

PANIC AT THE POOL

A smattering of applause as Anam reached the four-minute mark was replaced with looks of concern and apprehension when five minutes elapsed. Several of Anam's men exchanged glances. If Anam was well and they ruined his victory, they faced severe punishment. Finally, after waiting for six minutes, a pool attendant jumped into the pool and swam quickly toward the central pole. He dove and was surprised to see Anam's limp body, with his hand grabbing a handle. His eyes were open.

After releasing the gripped hand, the diver surfaced with Anam's body. He motioned to the rest of the crew, and they assisted in getting Anam out on the deck. A physician checked Anam's respiration, pulse, and heartbeat. There was no discernible breathing or vital signs. He applied aggressive external cardiac massage. A medic brought an oxygen tank with a face mask. After several minutes of cardiopulmonary resuscitation, Anam was pronounced dead. The people around the pool shouted in agitation. This was not something anyone had anticipated, and therefore, no maneuvers were practiced. Some delegates left the pool deck area and returned to their rooms. Others lingered, either out of morbid curiosity or genuine concern. A medical emergency squad arrived and placed Anam's body on a stretcher. He was transported to a nearby hospital.

The idea of a news blackout was untenable. This was not Baran, and therefore, Anam's security staff held no sway with the local media. A television crew appeared on the scene and approached Anam's personal physician, Dr. Ali Sharif, a tall, fastidious man in a French tailored suit. A bearded cub reporter asked, "What happened? Did he collapse as a result of the big dinner he had before the dive, or did somebody kill him?"

The doctor tried to explain the circumstances of the events that led to his death. "To my knowledge, Mr. Hafiz was reasonably healthy. He was taking mild medications for his high blood pressure. He had not had much to eat or drink because he knew he would dive that night. He, however, was a light cigarette smoker."

Another reporter, older and more established, asked for clarification. "Do you believe his death was the accidental result of the strenuous effort? What else could have happened?"

The physician elaborated, "Several things could have happened. Despite his protestation to the contrary, Anam was not an athlete. This endurance contest was an improvised event. It was ill-conceived and imprudent, but he wanted to impress the delegates to the convention. A middle-aged man, a smoker, with mild hypertension, and untrained, he was, nevertheless, passionate to win and prove his superiority. Naturally, such a man may suffer a heart attack, arrhythmia—that is to say, irregular heartbeats—stroke, or a vasovagal reaction, a collapse that may well precipitate his death. We will obviously perform an autopsy and check his blood and organs to establish, if possible, the cause of death."

The journalist dispensed with niceties. "Doctor, what I am asking you is, could he have been poisoned?"

Dr. Sharif raised his eyebrows in impatience. "My dear fellow, the food he ate and the drinks he imbibed were given to him by his loyal servants. Anyway, it was all shared with the other guests. To my knowledge, no one else has become sick. This is not the time or place for conspiracy theories."

A burly police officer nodded skeptically. "We will check the kitchen and all the personnel, as well as all the food and drinks the deceased consumed."

The exasperated doctor snapped his medical bag shut. "The autopsy and the toxicological analyses should shed some light as to the cause of death. There is no need for idle speculation."

A group of detectives inspected the pool's central pole and noticed nothing unusual. The remaining guests were told to return to their rooms and to make themselves available for possible questioning later that morning. The party was over, and the delegates would fly to their various homes during the course of the next few days. The news was transmitted locally and soon was seen worldwide. The reaction ran the gamut from dismay that a local strongman could die so mysteriously, eliminated possibly by his own people, to speculation as to the effect the dictator's untimely death would have on the price of gasoline.

CHAPTER 12

THE DEPARTURE OF THE TEAM

Hassan, Alex, and Simon were all watching TV from inside their separate limousines. So, even though Alex and Simon were traveling apart from Hassan and Eva, they all had access to the same news, transmitted by all the local TV channels. Hassan and Eva were fluent in Arabic and understood the culture of its speakers. This gave them the ability to properly gauge the mood on the streets. Alex and Simon, however, understood the language poorly and, therefore, were out of the loop. Alex asked the driver to switch to CNN. A TV newsman somberly reported.

"A poorly understood event is shaking world news. At the conclusion of the International Affairs Organization meeting, a summit hosting nations from both the East and the West, a farewell party was held at the Mera Hotel in Daman. The host was Anam Hafiz, the prime minister of Baran. Some sort of diving contest was announced, and the winner was to receive lavish gifts. Unfortunately, something unexpected took place. The last person to dive in the water was the host himself, Mr. Hafiz. After waiting more than five minutes for the leader to resurface, rescuers dove into the pool and pulled his lifeless body out of the water. Despite desperate attempts to revive him using CPR, Anam Hafiz was pronounced dead. His body was immediately transferred to a local hospital. The cause of death has not been determined. It is being speculated that he may have suffered a heart attack or other fatal event. The possibility of poisoning will be ruled out only after an autopsy is performed."

At this point Alex looked silently at Simon, who fidgeted nervously. Hopefully, they would avoid any last-minute complications. The news was repeated several times, and interviews with eyewitnesses, including the US ambassador, were transmitted. The Honorable Douglas Edwards, usually unflappable under the most trying circumstances, was visibly shaken.

"I . . . I had just congratulated Mr. Hafiz on his recent democratic reforms and the direction he was taking in leading his country, when . . . and, yes, we had come to an understanding on OPEC quotas. This is obviously unprecedented. We must get to the bottom of this and ensure a smooth transition, for the good of the people of Baran."

Alex smiled and told the chauffer to turn the TV off. Each limo arrived at the airport without incident. Hassan and Eva would be returning to the Bahamas, and Alex and Simon to the United States. Their flights were on time. Apparently, there were no suspicions of foul play yet, as all the delegates were allowed to transit freely within Daman. Ultimately, no one was detained at the airport, and all arrived safely to their respective countries. Hassan, Eva, Alex, and Simon saw each other only briefly after passing through security. They spoke little and said their quick good-byes. Alex's last words were terse.

"It's over. Nakba, catastrophe. We will meet again in the near future. Wait for a letter and the promised reward."

ABOUT THE AUTHOR

Byron Daring is the pseudonym of a young, imaginative author of numerous science-fiction books. Although his true name is not revealed, he has been a philosopher, a teacher of humanities, and a good friend of those who suffer. He has lived and traveled extensively throughout Europe, Africa, Asia, and the Americas; however, his current whereabouts are unknown. He has used his vast knowledge and his contacts with friends from exile to write this novel. Readers of this book should think about the suffering of those who live under oppressive regimes. We can always administer assistance to those in need, regardless of where we are and to whom we direct the help. We have an obligation to give back something of what we receive, and that is one thing we should always keep in mind.